I stand on the beach sometimes and holler across the waves.

And I don't think anybody even pays attention anymore. I've been doing it for so long that I can't remember when I didn't. So it came to me a while back that if I scream enough, he'll come back.

Is there a boy walking miles away listening to me as my screams sink from the air down to him?

One day, "Come back."

The next day, "Red."

The next one, "To me."

looking *for* red

looking *for* red

ANGELA JOHNSON

SIMON PULSE
New York London Toronto Sydney Singapore

First Simon Pulse edition November 2003

SIMON PULSE
An imprint of Simon & Schuster
Children's Publishing Division
1230 Avenue of the Americas
New York, NY 10020

Also available in a Simon and Schuster Books for Young Readers hardcover edition.
Designed by O'Lanso Gabbidon
The text of this book was set in Garamond 3.

Manufactured in the United States of America
4 6 8 10 9 7 5

The Library of Congress has cataloged the hardcover edition as follows:
Johnson, Angela.
Looking for Red / by Angela Johnson.—1st ed.
p. cm.
Summary: A thirteen-year-old girl struggles to cope with the loss of her beloved older brother, who disappeared four months earlier off the coast of Cape Cod.
ISBN-13: 978-0-689-83253-6 (hc.)
ISBN-10: 0-689-83253-2 (hc.)
[1. Brothers and sisters—Fiction. 2. Grief—Fiction. 3. African Americans—Fiction. 4. Cape Cod (Mass.)—Fiction.] I. Title.
PZ7.J629 Lo 2002 [Fic]—dc21 2001042846
ISBN-13: 978-0-689-86388-2 (Simon Pulse pbk.)
ISBN-10: 0-689-86388-8 (Simon Pulse pbk.)

For Nancy Church, who will be missed forever—A. J.

missing

1

When I was four, I could read the newspaper backward and upside down. I would stand and read the newspaper and not know I was doing it. Then suddenly everyone realized I was reading.

It was something that just happened to me. It wasn't strange or anything. Magic, almost.

So my brother, Red, started putting me on the back of his bike so I could read the store signs as we flew by. It was speed-reading on wheels. He could never go fast enough. I'd scream, "Pedal faster, Red. Pedal faster."

And he would, laughing the whole time.

It's Red who I think of every time I pick up a book, ride my bicycle, or hear someone laugh. Everything was always him. He was always there, and we were always us.

But then one day my brother, Red, just disappeared from us forever.

You never know.

Red.

It used to be just me and Red. All the seasons along the coast, and seabirds, lobster breakfasts, and the beach all day. There were many summers and so many jars of shells that if I ever left the ocean, I would still feel it in my bones.

But maybe it's Red that I feel. Maybe that's why I see him in the mirror and then I don't. Maybe I'm not really here, but someplace else where missing brothers walk past dinner tables unseen.

I'm lucky, though, 'cause when the house is quiet and my heart is aching, at least I feel something, and I don't have to leave here and go looking.

2

Once Red and I were caught offshore during a storm. We'd sat fishing in the little skiff that our dad, Frank, had fixed for us the summer before, catching so many porgies that both our buckets were overflowing. I remember my feet hung over the side of the *Daisy Moon* while Red told stories of sea monsters and how the old mapmakers used to think any place not charted on maps had dragons.

Red knew all kinds of sea stories 'cause he used to hang around Gloucester with Frank and his friends. Some, fishermen for a living, the others just living to fish. Frank would say that Red was learning the sea. . . .

Anyway, the *Daisy Moon* was rocking gently under a Cape Cod blue sky one minute, and about to capsize under ugly, dark skies the next. The following twenty minutes were some of the scariest of my life. Waves crashed and almost swamped us. Red pulled me into the middle of the skiff, tightened my life vest, and told me stories of mile-long fish that laughed and played water polo.

I remember I held on to Red and buried my head in his chest, listening to his heartbeat. I remember the cold. I remember Red's calming voice.

A calming voice at ten years old.

Suddenly there was Frank in the motorboat towing us back to shore.

I couldn't get warm for weeks. My mom kept blankets all over the house and filled me with hot cocoa. Red watched and told me stories about the hot desert and how they'd actually found fish bones where there wasn't any water that anyone could see.

It took me a while, but I finally got warm.

Red went back out the next day.

I stood on our widow's walk and watched as he pulled porgies out of the bay, waving to me. I worried that a storm would come up again, this time taking Red away forever and beyond.

It's seven years now since that cold, wet day.

3

My mom, Cassie, walks in looking tired.

"Sometimes I wonder why we live by the ocean," she says.

Then she drags in two buckets and some paintbrushes from the hall and throws herself onto the beanbag chair. Her braids fall across her face.

"Damn!" she says, closing her eyes.

She falls onto the chair like I do; like she's fourteen instead of thirty-five. Ageless. I think that's what you'd call Cassie. It makes me mad because I feel so old. So very old.

Sometimes I want Cassie to look tired and worn out. You know, like someone who can't take one more minute of whatever it is that's dragging her down. But she never looks that way. She never complains or feels like the end is coming.

She told me this once.

She said with a grin once that complaining and worrying was just not what she was about. And her eyes looked clear through me when she said that.

What you see is what you get with Cassie. Always.

"I love living on the Cape," I say. "Why would I ever want to wonder about living anywhere else but here?"

Cassie laughs and kicks the bucket over. It rolls along the floor and stops underneath the front window, which looks out onto the beach. She yawns and stretches out on the beanbag. In a few seconds she's asleep.

Asleep and snoring.

Frank says she slept while she was in labor. The nurses said they'd never seen anything like it. I hate that she sleeps that hard, that deep.

But I get up to cover her with the pink Mexican blanket we got last year in California. Now all her braids fall across her honey brown face; it's still moist from the outside humidity and sweat from whitewashing the fence.

I sit on the floor beside her and listen to the waves crash against the shore, and listen for something I'm not going to hear, because that's all in the time before now.

I watch my mother sleeping like a baby and I am alone.

Even though it's calmer on the water today than it was yesterday, I worry. I watch from the windows as little kids splash in and out of the waves. But for one minute—just one—I want to drag them all off the beach. I want to bring them all in the house and keep them safe, because when you grow up believing in dragons and the great beyond, you believe that they can show up anytime, taking anyone. My visions of dragons never go away.

Something I remembered.

Cassie promised this old aunt she had that she would dance on her grave when the time came.

I was so little when I heard Cassie say she would do this that I used to dream about spinning in the cemetery in a pink-and-white tutu. My hair would be pulled back in a bun, and the tights I wore would sparkle as I spun and twirled over the markers. I was a baby then and did not understand.

I'd sing, too.

I would dance and sing for all those who couldn't.

I would be like Cassie, who loved her aunt. Who loved to dance on Saturday nights even though she was Pentecostal and thought she would probably go to hell—dancing.

It is because of her aunt that Cassie doesn't have any religion. She says people like her aunt Charity were Nirvana-bound the second the doctor smacked them. Hell would melt if somebody like her aunt Charity ended up there.

I think she's right.

I feel she's right.

I know she's right.

But now I don't want to dance in a tutu in pink. And I definitely didn't want to sing. I told Cassie I didn't want to sing or dance on graves anymore like she might. And when she asked me why, I wouldn't answer.

4

I used to daydream that I could walk from the Atlantic to the Pacific in one day. I would start at our front door, heading west. I'd tromp down through the Delaware Water Gap and over the mountains. No problem.

It wouldn't be too hard to cross the Midwest. There'd be hundreds of miles of flatness, with me walking through it all, loving the plains. And when I got to the Rockies, I'd climb so very high I'd see California from them. I'd see the desert and smell lemons. Then I'd be there. The Pacific would be mild, blue, and smooth as I sat on the beach and let the warm breeze blow through me.

But I'd miss the Cape, you see. I always do. So I'd have to walk back that day. I would walk barefoot all the way back because I knew the land now.

The mountains and plains would be sure and friendly under my feet as I walked back home.

I slurp soup and listen to Frank and Cassie talk about the new houses going up in the neighborhood. They laugh and drop spoons at the table when they talk about how our neighbor Jo is taking it all.

Jo spies on the contractors. Change. She doesn't like it.

Cassie laughs. "When I last saw her, she was on the widow's walk with a pair of binoculars. Looked as if she even had a picnic lunch up there."

"Do you think she'll give in and go back into her house anytime soon?" Frank says.

Cassie chews bread and says, "Don't know. Everything's been hard on Jo since she got arthritis. A couple of years ago she would have walked up and down the building site with a picket sign."

It was Jo who taught Red to fish. I watched that quiet afternoon as they sat in the skiff out in the bay for hours. Reeling and just looking out over the water. Hours and hours in the gently rocking boat 'cause time out there just doesn't mean anything.

At least that's what Jo always says.

"Mike? Mike, you still with us?"

I nod and drag my legs into a crossed position, pulling the beads on my ankle bracelet.

Sometimes I forget my name is Michaela, 'cause nobody in the family has ever called me that. I relax in this position 'cause I can pull on the anklet, whose beads are sea blue and smooth.

They used to be Red's.

When he was three, beads were the only thing he ever wanted from the toy store. Cassie was warned not to give them to him—he was too young and would swallow them—but Cassie ignored it all. She said his face lit up like he was envisioning magic. So every birthday she got Red beads. He never stopped loving them.

He'd kept them in jars underneath his bed. We'd find them all through the house.

One day after Red disappeared Cassie was sitting on the living-room floor knitting when she spotted one of Red's beads. She looked like someone had punched her, and she started unraveling the sweater she was knitting.

But no tears. Not one.

She just vacuumed for the rest of the day.

Frank left after the fourth vacuuming and

walked down to the beach. I walked into Red's room and pulled one of the jars from underneath his bed and hid it in the back of my closet.

The next morning the rest of the jars were gone.

No more sea blue smoothness waiting. No more Red to come back to it.

"I'm still here," I finally say.

"You should go to Jo's. Talk and take her mind off this obsession with that building site," Cassie says.

"What's wrong with her mind being on it? Nothin' wrong with her feelings."

"You're right." Frank smiles.

"Nothing wrong at all, Mike," Cassie adds.

I look at my parents and know that they are mouthing words they know by heart. You know the ones—*don't judge anyone, let people feel as they will.*

Yeah, they know the words.

But I should still go to Jo's to keep her mind off the new houses and get her to focus on something not so crazy.

I watch Jo from our widow's walk. Her short gray hair blows in the breeze. I kneel and watch her take the binoculars from her face. She starts laughing.

I yell, "What's up?"

She waves at me and walks slowly back to the chair she dragged up to the walk.

She hollers, "They can't start up their heavy equipment."

"What happened?"

She cups her hand to her mouth. "It's probably the sea air. You never know about weather conditions around here. I've seen cars working perfectly just refuse to start up because of the salt air. . . ."

A gust of wind comes up and carries her word *air* away toward the water and out over the waves. I start to wonder if someone will step out of a door in England to go for a walk and suddenly hear, "air."

Would the word follow him on his walk?

Could he imagine the word had been stolen by the wind from across the ocean from a gray-haired fishing woman who drinks tea on her roof and may be a saboteur of earth movers?

He'd never know her or that she taught my brother to fish.

I yell back to Jo, who's sipping tea now, "The air up here can get you."

Then I turn toward the water and watch the sailboats glide on and out, and think about Cassie and Frank and how I never want to know words by heart when it comes to somebody else's feelings.

5

Red kept frogs.

Red kept frogs everywhere.

He said frogs knew what it was all about and what was going to happen to all of us if we didn't watch out.

Frank would always complain to Cassie that Red watched too many nature documentaries and wild-animal shows. Said he was growing up loving animals more than people. Cassie said she didn't see anything wrong with that.

She liked animals a whole lot better than people because they didn't hog two parking spaces when they'd bought overpriced cars, and didn't force other animals at gunpoint from their homelands or use lawyers as flamethrowers.

Cassie really meant the last part 'cause her

family was full of lawyers. She wouldn't admit it to most people, though. She loved her family when they weren't being lawyers.

That's why she married Frank. He wasn't a lawyer. He worked with his hands, and on their second date he told her he wanted thirty-two kids and twelve dogs. Thirty-two kids seemed like too much to Cassie, so she talked him down to twelve kids and six dogs.

Cassie said she had to marry the crazy man, 'cause who'd even joke about wanting that many babies. . . .

Red would have said frogs never thought about how many tadpoles they'd have.

People should keep blue beads out. On their floors. Around their windowsills, all over their houses.

Cassie sweeps around mine now.

Frank walks over them in his waders and work boots.

I lie on my belly, eye level, and go into them. Living in a blue-bead world with air bubbles just dancing through my head. I could lie there for hours. I do.

Frank sometimes puts my dinner beside me on the floor. I eat toasted cheese sandwiches and pickles in my blue marble world while Cassie and Frank talk and step over me.

When I stay the night somewhere else, I miss them, Red's blue beads.

I start looking for them.

I say I am going to the bathroom or need a drink of water, but what I am really doing is looking for blue worlds in closets and drawers. Anyplace could be hiding the beads.

I never find any.

Not one.

I want to ask my friends' mothers where the beads are. Do they hide them when people come over? Are they trying to keep them from me?

So one night at my friend Gia's house I woke up way after everybody in the house was asleep and went looking.

When Gia's dad found me, I was crying behind the couch. Then I was screaming at him. How they could live in a house without beads.

When Cassie came to get me at four that morning, Gia's mom told her that I was sleepwalking. She told Cassie about the bead "nonsense."

Frank put a warm blanket over me just as the sun was coming up over the Cape. I fell asleep in our house with a ring of sea blue beads around me.

6

I stand on the beach sometimes and holler across the waves.

And I don't think anybody even pays attention anymore. I've been doing it for so long that I can't remember when I didn't. So it came to me a while back that if I scream enough, he'll come back.

Is there a boy walking miles away listening to me as my screams sink from the air down to him?

One day, "Come back."

The next day, "Red."

The next one, "To me."

7

I think it's like walking barefoot in a room full of broken glass, when someone you love goes away.

You have to get out of it, so you have to go on no matter how many jagged pieces of glass stab you. Some pieces hurt more than others. Some make you think you ain't ever going to walk again. And you start saying to yourself, "What stupid person broke all this glass, anyway, and tricked me into the room?"

It's bad shit, and they say everybody just has to go through it.

I used to watch Frank and Cassie.

I wanted to learn how they did it. But they weren't any better than me at it, and I didn't like them for a long damned time because of it. They

should have known something. A secret. A pass-
word. A potion against the broken glass.

My aunt Caroline lives way out on the Point.
Alone.

Everybody calls her a witch, and they may be
right. They may be right.

I walk down the road past the blue gray houses
and the lighthouse on the hill. We used to walk to
her house every morning in the summer, shoeless,
carrying our bait pails.

That's why I'll miss the summer.

Me, Red, Caroline, and no shoes.

I could miss the summer for a lot of reasons,
but it all comes down to this.

She's waiting for me in her garden of sage and
peppermint and some plant she keeps by the front
gate that she says keeps out evil. She smiles when
I pull a leaf of peppermint.

"Hot day, Mike."

"Yep," I say.

"Got some new gear."

I smile and walk into the house, which is cool
and reminds me. Everything's been reminding me.
I drop to the floor and start looking over the fishing pole. Caroline goes into the kitchen and comes

out with iced tea and peppermint, and starts talking about where she got the fishing pole and how long it took her to pick it.

She looks like Frank, even though they have different moms.

And she is the only one who knows all about me.

Cassie and Frank don't say so, but they don't want me coming to Caroline's so much. It never used to be that way. They never cared before.

Now they watch me with big eyes when I go out the door and head off toward the lighthouse, and offer me rides downtown, or ask if I want to go hang out with my partners, Mark and Mona. Or do I want to go swimming, 'cause they're packing a lunch.

The water is almost warm on my feet when it comes over the dock. I cast my line into the gray green water. The ocean thunders, then is quiet. Caroline uses her old pole and I use the new one.

Lately it's only this and being surrounded by beads that makes me feel good.

Caroline's hat covers her eyes, and her long cotton dress is soaked up to her knees. The fish just come to her. Like magic. One after the other, forty in two hours.

I get a few and that makes me happy.

We keep on fishing, though, way into the day and well past afternoon, until Caroline says, "Hot day, Mike."

"Yep," I say.

"Some gear, baby."

I nod, and we pick up our fish and put our poles over our shoulders to walk back to the house that reminds me.

8

The first time I knew my brother, Red, was still around was the day Frank and Cassie broke down outside Boston with two flat tires. It's only now that I think that it was all Red's doing. He needed time to let me know that he is . . . Just us again.

Two flat tires. One after the other, and me at home waiting for them.

People see missing persons all the time and don't know that they are. They sit beside them at movies and shop beside them in stores and pass them on the street. You don't know these people, so how could you recognize that someone, somewhere, is missing them?

So I'm telling Caroline all about it now, 'cause who else would believe me?

Caroline says that her and Frank used to tell

each other stories that scared them so bad that they had to sleep with the light on.

The winter stories were scarier than the summer ones because of the quiet of the falling snow. Not a sound sometimes. Not one. And no kids running around late through the projects where they lived, ignoring their parents yelling for them to come into too-hot apartments for the night.

Caroline says that what my dad believed in then was no indication of what a doubting old man he'd turn into.

She said it real sad, like it was the worst thing in the world. She said—and let me get this right—that Frank used to suspend disbelief. Now he was just a disbeliever.

Caroline says that sometimes being old has to be just about the most boring thing in the world to be.

Now.

Now it's the beads and fishing with Caroline and not being home enough to be reminded.

Now it's sitting in the window looking out at the water, feeling Red within the waves, hearing him in the surf. Now is me not wanting to be anywhere or with anybody, or to know anything about what is going on in the world.

Before now was all the times with me and Red. Like the day before he disappeared, when I didn't know a damned thing about how life without him would be.

That day Red smoked a cigarette behind the garden shed and blew smoke rings at me while I tried to inhale them. When he saw me trying to inhale, he put the cig out with the heel of his boot and shook his head, smiling that Red smile at me.

I saw him again today, leaning against the garden shed. No cigarette, though. Red leaned against the north wall and looked relaxed. I sat on the back of the couch in the living room and looked down at him and knocked at the window to get his attention. I knocked for about ten minutes, until Cassie screamed that she would go out of her natural mind if I didn't stop that noise.

I wanted to tell her that Red was down there, standing against the shed.

Not smoking, like the last time I saw him there.

Not smiling, like the last time I saw him.

And not alive, like the last time I saw him there.

But he was gone.

9

Red's girlfriend, Mona, has big brown eyes and always puts her arms around me when I get close enough. She smells like powdered sugar and strawberry licorice.

"Sweet," Red used to call her. He said she was and always would be.

And he was the only one Mona said she would ever love, and she knew it once he was gone.

"Hey, beautiful thing," she calls to me as I am walking past the Ice Kreem Kastle over by the Tides Motel. She sits underneath a table umbrella sipping something and waving away flies.

"Come on over here and give me a hug."

I do.

"How you been, beautiful?" Then she puts her fingers down into her cup and flicks whatever it is at me.

I smile.

Mona stretches way back and closes her eyes.

"You should come around more, beautiful. I miss you. Just when I think that I'll never get over him, I see you. Then I *know* I'll never get over him."

I nod.

"What have you been doing lately?"

"Nothing."

"Me, too," Mona says. Then she starts to cry. "I've been thinking about leaving this place. Going someplace where the air is dirty and the people are gray and depressed."

I watch her.

"It might help to be with people like me, feeling like me."

I say, "Maybe," and she hugs me again before I can get away. She keeps on crying, though, and I've gone a block before I remember to say, "Take me with you."

I go out on the boat with Frank, and he drinks beers and fishes all day long. I don't know if he goes out onto the water to fish or to drink his beer, 'cause he doesn't drink in the house or anywhere else.

Just on the water.

I wonder if I'll be like him, quiet and kind—

drinking beer on a boat and remembering to smile at my daughter even when she doesn't catch any fish.

Tomorrow school starts. I will walk down the halls like everyone else, not knowing where I'm going.

Pritchard Howard (everybody calls him Nick) will lock a sixth grader from the middle school in his locker and leave him. I will walk past, listening to the kid scream—but I won't laugh like almost everybody else. But I won't let him out, either. (Later I'll probably cry, alone, about it.)

In homeroom Ms. Wallace (who has been on leave and out of the country for two years) will say to me, "I had your brother, how's he doing?"

Everybody will get quiet and there will be no movement in the room.

I will say, "He's doing fine, Ms. Wallace. Just fine."

And when I get to the cafeteria, there will be six empty tables. I will sit at the one farthest from the kitchen.

If I were in the Group, about ten kids would push past everybody to sit down beside me, talk real loud, and laugh at stupid-ass stuff that doesn't mean anything. I'd laugh with them, probably.

But instead, all the quiet kids and nontalking cybergeeks (with a seat between one another) will sit down at my table. We will look up from our food, books, laptops, or comics only to ask someone to pass the salt.

And I'll be fine there.

I will watch the gymnastics team sail through the air during independent study, with about twenty other people who have nothing to do.

Mona used to be a gymnast, but now she won't ever go to practice or even talk to her old teammates. I know this 'cause Meadow Sofer will tell me when she sees me in the library later.

"Talk to her, Mike. Tell her she should come back."

And all I will think is, *Why does this girl even think I know Mona?* But then I will remember that everybody knew Red, and I seemed to have stood in his light, so I must have reflected at some time.

Then she will go on about how Mona needs to take her mind off things and get back to normal.

It will be then that I remember the sixth grader in the locker, but I won't say what I want to say; which is none of us should want to be normal.

* * *

Caroline picks me up after school. She doesn't have to ask me anything about the first day. She doesn't say anything and it's probably a good thing, 'cause I cry all the way to her house.

I sail along, quiet on the skiff, and watch everybody on shore.

The summer people are gone and everything is back to normal. Sometimes I wonder how we can stand the wait. Waiting for the people to leave and the sunblock to leave the air. We're used to it, though.

Sorry to say, I am.

Sometimes I even miss them, the summer people. They were watchable and happy to be here. That's something, I guess.

Cassie is waving from the widow's walk.

I wave back, then close my eyes in case she wants me to sail in and isn't just saying hi. And I don't feel bad about it at all 'cause it's an I-don't-want-to-be-in-the-house day. That's what her and Frank call it.

I drift along, getting real close to the Vineyard, then decide to start back. I'll sit on the beach and eat dinner on the sand, knowing Cassie and Frank will join me. We'll all sit there sharing a sad family picnic. And maybe someone will watch us from the ocean and think we are happy late-summer people.

Sorry to say, they'd be wrong.

looking

10

Mark Hollywood crashed his car into the side of Nemo's Fresh Seafood last night. He broke his arm and left leg. Somebody said he purposely aimed for the center of the restaurant. I didn't believe it till I heard Mark say so himself.

I stood and watched while a bunch of people in orange tried to pry the car out of the Nemo's kitchen.

Mark ended up at Mercy Hospital on suicide watch.

I could have told them all that it wouldn't do any good to watch him. I could have saved them all the time and energy that it was going to take them to keep an eye on him while he lay there in pain. Mark wouldn't ever try it again.

I'd bet anything that I cared about.

Mark and Red used to jump off the pier into the bay. I used to hide behind the tall, whooshing willows and close my eyes until I heard the splash below them, then the whooping and screaming after they had made it back up out of the water—still alive.

I used to get this sick feeling all over as they flew off into the water. I was still a little scared of everything I couldn't see. And that included everything underneath the waves. They never asked me to come with them. Never.

Red said that it wasn't that he thought I'd be too scared. (I was.) He said it was something him and Mark always did together.

It was okay by me. I didn't really want to watch my brother jump off into nothing so far below.

Mark Hollywood wasn't afraid of anything. He used to jump off the pier faster than Red and scream louder when he came up. I thought he was something bigger than life. I didn't think anyone or anything could knock him down.

I guess I was wrong.

He looked pale and miserable in the hospital bed.

Caroline gave me a ride to see him at Mercy, and since she knew the nurse on duty, she talked to her while I went in to see him. Maybe he wasn't on suicide watch after all. He wasn't in the psych ward. That was something.

Mark smiled at me when I walked in.

"Hey, Mike."

I walked toward the bed real slow, like if I moved too fast, I might break another one of his bones.

"You okay, Mark?"

He nodded with his face all black and blue, then turned away and looked toward the window.

"Yeah, I'm fine. Just fine. Hell—I've never been better. How about you? How you doing?"

He looked me straight in the eye when he asked how I was doing, like I couldn't have been better than his broken, bruised self. I sat down in the chair beside him and grabbed hold of his hand. It felt rough in mine. It was bruised like the rest of him—even worse with the IV sticking out of him.

He squeezed my hand tighter when it looked like I might answer and held on to it like he was hanging on to a life raft. When I laid my head on the pillow beside him and inhaled so deep I thought I would pass out, he started to cry. Low and deep at first—then so fast and loud that it scared me.

I held my breath, waiting for him not to need to be that sad anymore.

Everybody knew Mark Hollywood had lived by himself for the last three years. Everybody knew he had a dad who nobody ever really saw and who always managed to be out of town selling something in another state since Mark's mom died.

The school never said anything.

The neighbors never said anything.

And there was no way any of the kids Mark hung out with would ever say anything, 'cause they were too busy having a good time hanging out in Mark's house, where no adult person had told anybody to do anything in the last three years.

But because Mark got good grades and never got caught doing anything that would get him put in juvie hall, everybody just closed their eyes to the boy who used to grocery shop with coupons and change the lightbulb over his garage when it blew out.

"He's a good kid," I guess they said.

I wonder if they would have worried more

about him if they had known he would eventually crash his car into a restaurant?

Would they have talked to his old man and told him that he shouldn't be punishing his own kid because his wife was gone?

Would they have cussed him out and told him he might as well just move out and leave Mark, for as much good as he did? But nobody ever did. And when Mark ended up in the hospital, nobody knew who or where to call for him.

Out of nowhere, though, Cassie was up at the hospital with phone numbers and insurance forms. Just like that. She shook her head at me as I stood beside her and almost asked her a question in front of the man admitting Mark to the hospital.

They wouldn't let me see him that night, so I went back home when Frank came to get me. Cassie sat up by Mark all night long. I didn't even think she liked Mark that much. I can't remember her saying more than a few sentences to Mark the whole time him and Red hung out together.

It went like this:

"Have dinner with us, Mark?" Yep.

"Want some lunch, Mark?" Yep.

"Bad weather out, Mark, stay over." Okay.

"Breakfast, Mark?" Yep.

But there she was, sitting up all night beside him.

When Cassie got back from the hospital the next morning, she almost looked worse than she did the night Red didn't come home.

She brushed past Frank before he could say or ask anything about Mark and went to her bedroom and slammed the door. Frank kissed me and walked out the door backward like he was waiting for Cassie to fly out of the room and drag him back to talk.

She didn't.

But she did cry hard. She cried so hard that I went to my room and surrounded myself with Red's beads 'cause I figured Mark Hollywood was dead.

When I asked Cassie a while later if he was dead, she only shook her head, then said, "No, girlfriend. Not yet."

That's when I decided that I had to see him. I remembered it all then. I knew that Mark hadn't crashed into Nemo's to kill himself and be with Red, like everybody but a few people thought.

The nurse woke me.

"Mark's downstairs getting tests. Do you want something to drink?"

I nodded and she brought me a ginger ale. I

sipped it and waited for Mark to come back. Just when I had really woken up, the phone rang. I picked it up.

Before I could say hello, a voice said, "Mark; be alive." It was Mona.

I whispered into the phone, "Mona—he is . . ." Then I hugged the phone to my chest and listened as the only other person in the world who knew that Mark wasn't trying to join Red cried hard into the phone while I listened for it all to go quiet.

It would have been easier to tell it all, to anybody, right then. It should have been.

11

We used to sit at the Center of the World and throw pinecones into the ditch on the side of the road. Red, Mona, Mark, and me would sit by the side of the road fighting off ants and swigging down cold sodas—no beers when I was around.

Nothing like sitting at the Center of the World and watching it all go by.

The tourists were always stopping to take pictures at the Center of the World sign. So if you looked in photo albums all across the country, you'd see us sitting under the sign, smiling and waving like we were the happiest people in the world.

Maybe we were. Maybe.

It's not something you really go around thinking about.

Do people think about how happy they are when they're walking the dog or hanging with their friends?

I didn't when we used to sit under the World sign and not even talk for hours.

I miss being, just being, with Red and everybody else. Now when I pass the sign, I can't even stop. I guess I can't really go back to the Center of the World ever again without my brother.

Mona pulls up in our drive and sits there for about twenty minutes.

I don't go out, and nobody in the house goes out either. We all know better now.

Because Mona hasn't come to see any of us. She hasn't come to pick anything up or drop anything off. She's come to soak up Red. She's been doing it since after the funeral. We got used to her sitting in the driveway looking up at Red's bedroom window, mouthing some song from the radio.

Jo, who always thinks something's up at first, said she was waiting. When I asked waiting for what, she just shook her head like she hadn't come up with that part yet. So I waited too.

Other people on our street started noticing Mona's red '65 Malibu parked in front of our house. Now they stop and talk to the sunglassed girl with her feet and red toenails hanging out the passenger window.

Frank said Mona parked in front of the house was like most things in life: If you did something enough times—even if it seemed strange, but didn't hurt anybody—everyone would just start to accept it. His real words were: "Eccentric behavior is the cornerstone of this country."

I watch Mona as her head bobs up and down in time to whatever music is on the radio. She never turns it up loud. She wouldn't want to bother anybody.

I watch for Red, too. He hasn't been leaning against the back shed or anything else lately, and I'm starting to think I was imagining him. But it doesn't matter if I did. The important thing is I got to see him.

When I look back to Mona, she's standing beside her Malibu, waving up at me in the window. And since she's never done that in all the time she's been sitting and waiting in the drive, I just stand there like a fool for a while. I guess it hits me that she's waving for me to come on out.

I do.

"Hey, beautiful thing."

I lean on the car and smile at her.

"Hey," I say.

Mona hops up on the hood of the car and looks off into the water, then smiles at me. "Wanna go for a ride?"

"Yeah."

"Wanna go for a fast ride with all the windows down and the radio blasting?"

I walk beside the Malibu and look off into the water too.

"I guess so," I say.

Mona is already in the car, revving the engine. Frank and Cassie are at the window that I looked out of a few minutes ago, and for a second, just a second, I think I see Red standing beside them looking off into the water.

We fly along the coast road, singing to the radio. It's bright today.

Mona wouldn't get caught without her sunglasses on. I never wear them, but I'm starting to think it might be a good idea, 'cause as it is now, I'm just about blinded in the car.

I miss Mona. Even though she's been sitting in front of our house for a couple of months, I haven't really talked to her that much.

We talk more when we run into each other accidentally on the street. I think she looks different. She doesn't float anymore. She used to float when she walked, just like she did when she did the vault in gymnastics. But now her neck is strained, and her whole body tenses to the beat of the music.

"How's it been going, beautiful? Am I asking you that too much?"

"No, you're not asking me it too much."

Mona pulls out a cigarette and smiles at me again. "I've been watching you at school, beautiful thing. I've been watching you when you think that you are alone."

"You have?"

"Yes."

Mona inhales deep and long. "You walk through school like you are taking part in a play. Did you know you do that?"

I stick my head out the window and let the air blow through me. I open my mouth and taste the ocean. I can't get enough of the salt. When I was really little, Red had to keep me from drinking the salt water. I'd gulp a mouthful when he wasn't looking. I used to think it was better than apple juice.

Red used to say that meant I must have been some sort of fish or something. I think that he might have been right about that when I was little. Now the only thing I want to do as far as the water is concerned is look at it.

"I see him, you know? I see Red everywhere and I think that I'm losing my mind."

I don't say anything 'cause it's too scary to think that maybe Red isn't just in my imagination.

"You know why I don't do gymnastics anymore?"

I knew I didn't have to answer her.

"Red wouldn't leave the gym. He'd just stand there watching me. I never knew when he'd show up. I don't think I would have minded so much if we had been alone. But he'd never show up when we were alone. It's like he didn't trust me or something. I finally had to stop gymnastics."

Mona pulls the car onto a beach that says PRIVATE—NO TRESPASSING. She never did understand how people could own the beach. So she made it a habit of crashing any beaches with No Trespassing signs on them.

I've been kicked off a few beaches with Mona, so I don't mind walking onto the dunes with her.

We walk hand in hand to the edge of the shore and watch the tide come in.

Mona lets go of my hand after a few minutes and runs into the water. I watch her kick and run in the water. I think it is the first time I've seen her happy in months. She acts like little kids do when they play in water.

I wish I could play like her. Laugh like her.

Mona is yelling something at me. I guess I was daydreaming again, 'cause I didn't hear her at all. She was like a silent movie—dancing in the water.

I think I hear her say, "He's out there!"

I stand up and cup my hand to my ear and yell, "What?"

Mona stands staring at me as the tide comes in around her, and doesn't say anything else. She turns her back to me and lets the water throw her wherever it wants. Sometimes when she is twirled around toward me, I see a big smile on her face. A couple of times it's almost like she's talking to somebody. Then she laughs.

I fall asleep in the sun with the water crashing against the sand and don't seem to need Red's blue beads to sleep.

He's close enough to me here, I guess.

* * *

Mona wakes me, dripping cold water and laughing.

We run back to the car and watch the sun go down.

"Do you know why they call this the Center of the World, beautiful thing?"

I lean back against the sign and blink into the oncoming headlights. "I never did know why they called it that."

Mona leans against me and whispers, "It's called the Center of the World because it is."

12

I was on my way to school one minute, but the next I was throwing rocks off the Cape bridge and thinking about how I shouldn't even try to get to school now because I'd missed first period anyway, and you know how it is when you come in in the middle of a class—you're lost in it for the rest of the time.

Caroline is sitting cross-legged on the dock with her back to me and her hands raised over her head.

And I know she hears me—as usual—when she says, "No school today?"

I take off my shoes and throw my backpack in the sand and hope my juice box hasn't exploded all over my extra T-shirt and candy bars.

I walk toward Caroline and have a flash of Red in my mind. . . .

We are standing on this dock and he's holding my hand. But the strange part is I'm a little baby and he's the age he was when he disappeared three months ago. I know it's me, though. I know it in my stomach, and just as I'm beginning to wonder how I could have turned into a baby that fast the whole vision is gone and I'm standing on the dock again, walking toward Caroline.

I sit so close to my aunt I smell the ocean on her.

A breeze blows across the Cape and makes me feel better about everything that I just imagined. I didn't want to feel any worse about it all.

Caroline asks again, "School canceled?"

"Yeah."

"Did it blow up, or fall into some kind of sink-hole?"

"Sinkhole."

"Was there a tragic loss of lives?"

"Not many. A few of the white mice in the biology lab who have been living on soda and chips got liberated. A few of the teachers who have been trying to retire for about twenty years were seen climbing out and faking injuries so they could get early retirement."

"Sounds like a nightmare."

"Not too much of one."

"Good thing you escaped without a scratch."

"It was a close call, but I've always been lucky that way."

Caroline gets up and turns toward me, smiling. "Oh yeah, baby, you have always been the lucky one."

And I don't even feel bad that the other side of that is my brother ended up being the one who wasn't lucky. The way Caroline says it, though, makes me feel warm and at the same time makes me want to give up my luck.

'Cause I'd do anything, anything, to have Red back.

Caroline puts her arm around me and we walk toward the house. Caroline leans down and picks off a piece of rosemary as we go through the garden gate. She inhales deeply and holds me closer because I've made up my mind. I'm going to spend the rest of the day with her.

There are baby pictures of everybody in our family from the last 120 years on the tables in Caroline's front room.

They are dark, old faces that must have been

looking up into the bright New England summer sun, because they all have squinting smiles. Most of the old pictures are serious ones.

Our family was full-bodied women with babies on their hips and about eight or nine other kids around them with hoops and bare feet in the Cape sand. The men wore suspenders at play and thigh-high waders. They carried nets and had slickers on.

Men of the sea.

Frank says that the family has been in the water forever, and I like to think of their dark, long-ago faces standing on fishing boats, weathering the storms that came in from the north and gave the widow's walk its name.

I've been in Caroline's house a lot, but I've never looked real close at the photos of the ones who were here before we were. That is probably why I haven't ever seen the boy on the beach holding the little baby's hand.

I lean closer, and just as I realize the boy in the picture looks so much like Red, he could be his twin, I hear something hit the floor in the kitchen. It's loud enough to make me jump.

Caroline glides through the living room holding a broom.

"Broom fell. Company's coming," she says.

We both look at each other and think that the company probably has something to do with me and the school that in my dreams is sinking slowly into a hole.

I listen on the stairs as Frank paces up and down the floor of Caroline's front room.

"You have to stop coddling her, Caroline."

Caroline isn't talking, but is sitting with her arms crossed on the old cedar chest that my grandma left her.

"How is she going to start dealing with this if you keep sheltering her against it all?"

Caroline still isn't talking to him.

"She has to go to school."

Caroline shakes her head.

"Well, she does. Kids go to school, Caroline. They go to school. They have friends. They do things. They keep on going."

Caroline gets up and walks across to the picture window looking out onto the ocean and says, "How is she supposed to get on with it, Frank? Is she supposed to snap her fingers and stop missing her brother? Is she supposed to make believe, or go through all of this in a timely fashion?"

Frank looks at my aunt Caroline for a minute, then sinks right to the floor.

I close my eyes 'cause I don't want to see him cry again. I don't want to see his shoulders shake the way they did when we all stood on the boat in the bay, looking lonely and thinking about Red.

So I close my eyes and don't have to see Caroline leaning toward Frank and whispering something that I don't hear.

Everything is easier if you close your eyes.

13

I wake up crying.

I do it a lot lately.

I think that I will never get it all out of me. I think I will never be the person I was.

I wonder if Mona and Mark wake up not knowing where they are or when it will ever be the same again.

We are the only ones who saw him go.

And what could be harder? What could be worse?

14

Jo is kneeling in her front garden, cussing.

She's good at it and even taught me a few words when I was about four. I saved them up for just the right time. It was worth it to share them with everybody at a neighborhood picnic. Cassie and Frank just stared at me when I shared my new words with the pastor of the Presbyterian church. Jo fell on the ground laughing.

I lean against her wooden front gate.

"Weeds, Jo?"

She stands up and smiles like it's the best thing in the world to see me. It makes my shoulders go down, and my stomach stops hurting.

"If I could live on a planet without a damned weed invading my space, I'd be the happiest thing there. It wouldn't matter if it was a planet with just myself for company."

I smile and let her go on about the weeds. After a while she looks up again and laughs. "I haven't even invited you in. Come on. We'll have something cold to drink and something sweet and disgustingly bad for us to eat."

It's another world in Jo's house. She's proud to tell anybody who'll listen that none of the furniture has been moved in eighty-five years. Everything is just like her grandmother left it before she went off to live with a group of suffragettes in Philadelphia. Her grandfather raised her mother and uncle. Her grandmother was never welcome in the house after she left.

Jo says her grandfather was an old bastard who made his kids miserable old people before they were even in their twenties.

I like the way the silk feels on my legs as I sit in the high-backed chair by the front window. It swallows me, and I almost fall asleep before Jo comes back with the hot sweet tea and biscuits smothered in butter and blackberry preserves.

I stuff my face and swig the tea.

I don't have to talk when I'm at Jo's. She says people talk too much anyway. I relax and look out the window.

Jo does the same, and we spend most of the

Saturday afternoon watching the gulls steal food from the trash cans lining the beach.

Jo gets up after a while and takes the dishes away. We've done everything but lick the plates clean of jam. I take the teapot and cups into the kitchen behind her. When I get there, she's watching our backyard and shaking her head like she doesn't believe what she sees.

"What in the . . ."

I walk up behind her quietly and touch her shoulder. "Do you see him?"

Jo says nothing, only sucks in a bunch of air like she hasn't breathed in years.

I ask again, "Do you see him, Jo?"

When she finally turns back to face me, her eyes are wide and her hands are shaking. I take the flowered plate that held the biscuits we just ate, 'cause it looks like she might drop it right there.

Jo moves slow but finally sits down at the big, round kitchen table.

"Did you see him?"

She reaches across the table and holds my hand.

"Yes, I saw him." She looks at me, then lets go of my hand.

"Was he leaning against the shed and smoking?"

"He was."

"Was he staring up at the house or just look-ing off into space?"

"Staring at the house."

I pull my chair up next to Jo's. I've never seen her scared. She screams at town meetings and points her finger at developers and maybe even destroys private property. I didn't think anything could shake her.

Her face finally relaxes.

She goes over to the cupboard and pours some-thing from a clear bottle into a juice glass. She takes three drinks and sighs, leans against the cab-inet, and asks me, "Who else has seen him?"

I say, "I don't know."

She takes another drink and shakes her head slowly. "If I look out this window again, child, will he still be there?"

I say, "Maybe."

I guess she decides against it.

I walk over to the window, but Red is gone. I wonder where he goes to when he's not leaning against the shed. I wonder all the time.

"He's gone. I figured he wouldn't stay there long, since I'm not there."

Jo pours the rest of her drink out and walks

over to me. She wraps her arms around me and puts her face next to mine. There's a picture of us taken when I was three with her doing the same thing. She says I had just found some dead fish on the beach and started crying. A friend of hers snapped the picture.

"Do you think your brother is haunting you, Mike?"

I close my eyes 'cause I know the truth but don't want to see Jo's face when I tell her.

"His going away is haunting all of us."

"Who's all?"

"The three of us. Me, Mona, and Mark."

Jo whispers into my ear, "Why do you think that?"

I pull away from Jo and head for her back door. She doesn't come after me and I'm glad. I don't go to my backyard but head out down the coast road. Away from why I think it is and why that might be.

I walk only a few more minutes before I almost run headlong into Mark standing on the bridge. It doesn't surprise me at all when he says, "I wondered when you'd get here."

And it's even less of a surprise when Mona drives up and parks her car on the side of the road and walks toward us.

Mark leans against the bridge, and I finally notice the cast under his jeans and on his hand. Sunglasses hide his eyes, like they do Mona's. I should start wearing them, then I wouldn't have to worry about everybody looking sympathetically into my eyes.

"Hey," Mark says to Mona.

"Hey," I say too.

Mona walks over to the side of the bridge.

"What up?" But she doesn't sound that easy. She wants it to be light and easy, all of us meeting on the bridge.

It's not.

How could it be?

And whatever made us all come here at once isn't going to be talked about. 'Cause we all know, and there ain't no way of getting past it. It's all about Red, and nothing we do from now on can change any of it.

Not one damned thing.

15

Mark says when he was in the hospital he had a dream.

He and Red were climbing up a mountain in the rain. Mark wanted to stop and wait out the storm, but Red thought that they should keep climbing because the weather would get worse before it got better.

Mark finally stopped.

Red went on.

Mark is humming a song that I've been humming for the past week, and it's only this morning that I got it out of my head.

I sit next to him and Mona while we swing our feet off the bridge, throwing pebbles that we picked up from beside the road down into the water. And even though we are way above the water, I can see the ripple as the pebbles drop into the current below.

"Damn, that's a long drop," Mark says.

Mona blows a bubble and scratches the daisy tattoo on her ankle. Red and her got their tattoos together. He got one on his arm—poison ivy. I wanted one, and Cassie said that if I still wanted one in a couple of years, I could go to it. She hoped I'd get bored with the idea, but I didn't and sneaked off a few days later and got a dove on my stomach.

Cassie still doesn't know about it.

"Yeah, it's making me sick," Mona says.

"I like it," I say.

Mona and Mark look at me, then at each other. But they move closer to me when I lean my head over the rails.

Mona says she had a dream last week.

She was standing on the side of a mountain, and as Red reached the top she pulled him the rest of the way to his feet. Red wanted to get out of the storm, but Mona thought the rain felt good against her face, so she told him to go on.

I think about our dreams.

I think about how it would be so easy to sink underneath the railing and dive into the cool water.

Mark says, "It would kill you instantly."

"You'd be gone before you hit the water, girl-friend," Mona says.

"I know I could do it. I wouldn't even get bruised."

"Don't ever," Mona says.

Mark just looks at me real sad and shakes his head.

"It wouldn't be so bad. I've always wanted to high-dive."

"Well, you can just forget about it, Mike. It's crazy to want to jump from this height," Mark says.

"Just like it's crazy to crash your car into Nemo's, huh?" I say.

Mark looks out into the ocean and starts humming again. "You know why I did it."

"I don't," I say, 'cause he's made me mad and he's treating me like a baby.

"You know, Mike. Don't say you don't."

Mark has tears in his eyes and I'm sorry all of a sudden. Mona looks at me out of the corner of her eye and shakes her head. She leans past me and holds on to Mark's arm.

It doesn't make sense, but I feel jealous, for Red. Mona and Mark shouldn't ever care about each other, because Red is who brought them together.

But Red had left us all.

I get up and start walking down the road.

I turn and see that Mona and Mark are looking at me like I'm about to fall off the bridge. I turn and run, then realize that Mona is running after me.

She catches me, and I remember the first time I saw her run to fly off the vault in gymnastics. I sat next to Red while he looked at her like there was no other person in the world. I remember this and slow down to let her catch me just as I step off the bridge.

She says, "It's all going to be all right. All of this is only a dream. It's all just a dream. It's all just a dream."

I say, "Is it?"

"Yeah, it is."

"Then that's okay," I say.

And it is okay as she walks me back to where Mark is standing. There're wrinkles in his forehead, and I think that maybe he's in some kind of pain.

Mona starts walking me to her car. Mark follows, squeezing into the backseat after Mona and me have sat in the front seat for about five minutes.

I love the way the ocean smells just around sunset.

In late summer the smell of sunblock and french fries from the Potato Hut on the beach has been blown away by the sea breezes coming in across the Cape, and the sunset is an orange-and-purple, big-sweatshirt, deck-shoes-and-sweet-coffee-at-Bea's-Diner-to-beat-the-chill-in-the-air kind of thing creeping across the sky.

Mona starts up the car and drives toward the Center of the World—away from the sunset.

I dreamt last night.

I was in a little house in the woods and someone was knocking on the door. When I opened it, Red was standing in the rain. When I told him to come in, he only stood there. When I finally begged him to come in, he turned around and walked off into the dark, rainy night.

16

Mark can't ever go back into Nemo's, and he says that's a shame.

He used to get a bag of clams and three lemons and eat so much he could barely move. Him and Red loved clams.

Clams make me sick, but that doesn't stop me from going into Nemo's to get Mark a sack of them. The girl behind the counter, Pritchard Howard's sister, looks at me strange for a minute, can't place my face, then hands me the clams. I run before she calls Nemo out front and he ties me to Mark.

Around the corner Mark is sitting on top of Mona's Malibu.

"Thanks, kid," he says when I give him the clams.

He throws them down real fast, holding out the sack to me and Mona a few times. We both shake our head and lean against the car.

"These things are good," Mark laughs, and finishes off the bag. He doesn't look like the kind of person who just a few weeks ago everyone thought was trying to kill himself.

Even though he wasn't.

In the hospital when he found out that he was on suicide watch, he laughed at the doctor. So it wasn't going to matter what *anyone* thought about him.

I knew that Mark was keeping his part of the deal. He couldn't go back on his part, 'cause he could never make it up to the person it was made with. He could never make it up to Red.

I am comfortable where I am. Just this very second. Just this very moment. If nothing ever changed and I could stay this way forever, I'd be okay. It's hard to tell if Mona and Mark feel the same way, 'cause they're arguing about something I haven't heard them talking about. In a few minutes, though, they're laughing and smoking.

Mark looks at me. "What's wrong, Mike?"

Mona answers for me. "Probably nothing she can talk about."

She's right. It makes her put her cigarette out,

though. She's been complaining about her own smoking. She tried to get Red to quit.

"Nasty things," she says.

"Expensive things," Mark says, then picks up her half-finished smoke and puts it in his pack.

I'd been thinking about smoking until Red said thirteen was way too young to be so damned suicidal. Then he spent the afternoon blowing smoke in my face.

That was enough for me.

Mark stands up on the hood of the Malibu, pulls out the half-smoked cigarette, lights it, and inhales.

"Hey, you!" Nemo's seen Mark.

"Yeah," Mark mutters, and looks over top Nemo's head.

Nemo walks close to Mark. His hair is silver and he's one of the tallest people I've ever seen. Seven feet easy. He never smiles, but he never hollers at anybody either.

Mark leans back against the Malibu, favoring his leg. I wish he'd wear shorts more, 'cause I'd like to paint a mural on his cast. I've been trying to talk him into it.

Nemo looks at me and Mona and nods before

he speaks. "I know you kids have had a hard time. Sorry 'bout that." Then he looks at Mark real hard. "But that's no reason to take it out on my store."

The fish store looks like new now. Better. It smells lemony and clean—probably for the first time since it's been there.

"I wasn't taking anything out on your store, Nemo."

"It just happened, huh?"

"Yeah."

"Just like that?"

"Yeah, Nemo. Just like that."

Nemo looks at Mark's leg and arm, then the cuts on his face. "You're okay now, though?"

"Fine," Mark says.

Nemo looks at Mark real sad. Mark said once that Nemo and his dad had been in the same class in high school.

"It's just that you shouldn't give up, kid. Life can bite. Can't it? I mean, I know it does."

Mark listens. He doesn't try to explain about the deal, about Red, 'cause what would it all mean to anybody but us?

Then Nemo drops his long neck and turns red, like he's embarrassed that he said anything. Maybe he's sorry he told us life can suck, like he's taken our innocence away or something.

Mark limps toward Nemo and pats him on the back, and I think back to a time when I used to feel innocent. A time when I used to feel as young as I am. Mona almost smiles and puts her arm around me as Mark walks Nemo back to his store.

"It's okay, Mike. It's all right if they all think like Nemo. We don't have to explain. They never have to know."

But it's just like Mark said; it's all a shame.

Everything that happened then, and everything that will happen now.

listening

17

Midnight. Pitch black. The moon is hidden behind thick clouds that drew into town today and blocked out the sun everybody was expecting.

The last days of summer . . . you just have to have bright sunshine. Every little bit of sun makes everybody look up and smile. But it's black now, and the only way I even know that Mona is sitting on top of her car in our driveway is the red, glowing tip of her cigarette.

I raise my window up real soft 'cause I'm holding beads in my hand and don't want to drop them. I lean out and inhale salt and thick night air. And since the lights are out all over our house, I can stay with Mona and not worry about her, worrying about me, as I keep her company sitting in my window.

18

A story.

When Red was nine and I was six, we ran away to become fishermen. Really, Red ran away, and by the time he realized I was following him, *we* had run away, 'cause we were so far from the house that he didn't want to take me back.

I wish I could remember what made my brother want to run off and be a fisherman. I can't and sometimes think that if I could, I'd have some kind of clue about every damned thing in the whole wide world. But I can't remember, so this is just a story.

Frank says we were gone for three days.

Cassie says four, but by the second day they had pretty much drugged her up so much she couldn't recall anything if she tried.

One of the things I remember, though, is that I took the note that my brother left my parents. On it was a map of where he was going to be a fisherman. Hell, I remember saying to myself that I needed that map in case I couldn't keep up and got behind. Never thought—until now—how we probably would have been back that night if I'd left the note alone.

But all that didn't matter, 'cause I was going to be a fisherman just like Red. And Red was going to be a fisherman just like the picture of our great-grandfather, who Red was nicknamed after, hanging in the upstairs hall.

They looked exactly alike. So much so that Cassie used to show everybody who visited the house.

Red always smiled at the picture of the man who had been dead almost one hundred years before he was born. And he used to say, "I'm going to be just like him."

That's why he started hanging with Frank and his buddies in Gloucester and with Jo off the Cape.

You'd think with everybody pushing Red along fishing, there shouldn't have been any reason for him to leave home to do it, but like I said, his running off was for a reason I don't remember, so it wasn't about fishing.

So we slept on the beach the first night. We waited for everybody to take their umbrellas and beach towels in, then we put our sleeping bags down on the beach with the duffel Red had stuffed with sardines and saltines.

The moon was full that night, so we didn't even need the flashlight Red had brought. I remember how Red tucked me into his sleeping bag and went to sleep with his Walkman in his ears beside me. He never yelled at me for messing up his new career or slowing him down.

Two things happened that night.

First, the ocean sounded like wild horses running over metal roads and scared me half to death.

Second, the first Red stood at the edge of the water in his slicker and gun boots, watching us as we slept. I knew it was him and told Red in the morning that our great-granddaddy had protected us in the night. I realized later that I never thought to wake my brother up.

I remember that Red smiled at me.

He never told me I was imagining anything or making it up. He just smiled, opened a can of sardines, and told me to eat more than I gave to the gulls. Then we hid the sleeping bag and duffel under one of the houses near us and stayed on the beach the rest of the day. Red fished from the pier with a lot of other kids, and I splashed in the water when I wasn't sitting next to him.

I remember that the sun was so warm and bright that I fell asleep on the pier beside Red.

I remember that Red had a big iced soda sitting next to me when I woke.

I remember that the fish we didn't cook on the beach grills we gave to the gulls.

And finally, I remember that kids didn't tell. When the cops went along the piers and beaches with pictures of us, none of the kids said anything 'cause they knew we were fine, having just shared a bag of salt-and-vinegar chips with us after we'd come from the arcade.

The second night we slept underneath the pines out by the lighthouse, and I could see the light from Caroline's house. Later she asked me if the light had made me feel better. I just looked at her 'cause how did she know? How did she know?

Old Red came back that night.

He sat on the stump of a tree not fifty feet from me and my sleeping brother. In the almost full moon his molasses, crinkled face smiled at me and mixed with my dreams as I fell into a sleep so deep Red had to shake me awake the next morning.

Running away with a ghost.

When I told Red the old man had come back, he said at least we didn't have to feed him, then he grabbed my hand and marched me out of the trees to do more all-day fishing.

The large number of summer people made it easy for us to get lost in the crowd. We mixed with their kids and the busloads of people walking along the beaches.

It's easy to get lost in the summer here, and we did.

I can't remember who finally turned us in, but I don't think it was a big surprise or anything to Red. We got taken home by the cops and got to ride in the back and fly through the streets with the sirens blasting.

Frank was standing in the front yard when we pulled up, and after he'd hugged us, he said something about how he hoped this police and siren thing wasn't foreshadowing our future.

Cassie cried for about three days and didn't let us out of her sight for the rest of the summer, until Frank said we'd probably leave again if she kept us prisoners.

A little while after that she sent us to the store for bread.

But all this is just to let you know. They've been hanging around here for a long time. The ghosts. So it isn't so unbelievable that they're around us now.

But I guess not everybody would believe what I just said. They'd call it the imagination of a child. A story.

19

I wait for Mark on the front porch of his house, picking dead leaves from the pots he set out earlier this summer. Me and Red watched as he fertilized the soil and potted flowers for hours. Red was almost hypnotized as Mark named each one.

"Soapwort."

"What?" I jump 'cause Mark's walked up on me so quiet that he's nearly scared me out of my skin.

"That plant is called soapwort. It was my mom's favorite. She used to put it in pots all over the house. Said she wanted to look at it all the time and she couldn't do that outside. It's finished now. Only blooms for a couple of months. I need to take them out of the pots and put them in the rock garden."

I look at Mark as he limps across the porch and waters something by the front door, and think how everybody is afraid of him. They think he's some kind of thug who doesn't have anybody to tell him different.

He's not, but I think he likes people believing it.

I see his point, 'cause the world leaves Mark Hollywood way alone.

After a while Mark puts the watering can down and waves me into the house. I don't think I've ever been in a cleaner place in my whole life, except maybe a doctor's office.

"Want a soda?" Mark says.

I do and sit down on a couch that is so soft it almost swallows me whole. I look at all the framed pictures of Mark from when I didn't know him so good. He is about three in a picture where he's sitting on his mom's lap and smiling into the camera. In the bottom right corner somebody has written "Dublin, Ireland—1986." His redheaded mother smiles too.

And right next to that picture is an almost identical one of his dad holding him. "New Haven, CT—1986" is written in the corner of that one. Also, "Hollywood Family Reunion."

Mark says, "See, I really am black Irish," as he

nods at his black-skinned dad and pale white mother, then sets the soda on the coffee table in front of me.

I smile but don't get it.

Mark smiles back but doesn't try to explain it to me.

We sit in the cool quiet and don't talk for a while.

"Do you still cry for Red?"

I look at Mark real close and wonder how he knows I cry at all.

I say nothing.

Mark closes his eyes and starts humming (again) a song Red used to sing all the time, and it makes me want to start crying right there. I can't, though, 'cause no matter how close Mark and my brother were, I'm embarrassed to cry alone with Mark Hollywood.

Mark soon stops humming. "They towed my car to Vedders. I guess it's a total loss."

"I guess so," I say.

"It's not mine anymore, Mike."

"I guess not."

"I think that takes care of my part, don't you think?"

I drink the last of my orange soda and look off at the pictures of Mark, his traveling father, and long-dead mother and wonder if he cries for them anymore.

Mark leans closer to me and asks again, "Don't you think?"

I lean closer to him and still don't answer, 'cause it's hard to admit when you don't know.

20

Mona is waiting after school for me.

Radio blasting.

"Get in," she screams at me over the bass. Everybody looks at me. They want to be me, with a high schooler picking them up, blasting music and smoking so much I cough as I slide across the leather seat.

Mona takes off and I'm just me again—somebody no one in their right mind would want to be.

"What you been doing, beautiful thing?"

"Nothing."

"Nothing's good," Mona says as she passes a pickup truck along the Cape road.

"I saw Mark yesterday."

"Yeah."

"Yeah," I say, rolling my window down and putting my arm out to feel the air.

"How's he doing?"

I watch everything blow by so fast I realize that Mona must be doing about ninety. I must get real big-eyed staring at the speedometer, 'cause she starts slowing down.

"Sorry, beautiful thing."

"Mark says that he thinks his part might be done. His car's a wreck at Vedders and doesn't belong to him anymore."

"Oh, yeah?" Mona says as she lights up another cigarette. "What do you think?"

I cross my arms against my chest. "Why are you two asking me?"

Mona looks at me and slows down even more. It's only when you're sitting real close to her that you can see she's lost a lot of weight. Cassie thinks she's probably down to eighty-five pounds and worries about her.

Mona's face gets crinkled and she fights crying. "I didn't mean to upset you. I guess we shouldn't be asking you at all."

I know she means it and feel bad for acting like a baby. "Sorry."

"Me, too," she says, and keeps on driving. After we've gone about twenty miles, Mona really starts to slow up. We are in the deep woods; or at least it seems that way to me. Mona drives in what looks like circles, but in the end we come up on a building. The Milliet Institute. Mona takes one last drag of her cigarette, puts it out in the ashtray, and says, "Let's do it."

It's cool and dark when we walk through the wooden doors of the institute, and for a minute I don't know what the place is.

I hear "institute" in my mind and I think, *Whoa! Not me. Not yet. I'm not there yet.* But in smaller writing on the door it says, OCEANOGRA-PHY RESEARCH. I feel better about it, but I still don't know why Mona has brought me here, even though the lines in her face have smoothed.

Ernie Moffet wears a white coat and smiles at us when we walk into his office, so I guess he's expecting us.

He says, "Hi, I'm Ernie, and I'll be taking you on a sea adventure."

I start to giggle because he sounds so funny, like one of those people on kid science programs. He even looks like one.

Mona cuts her eyes at me and shakes her head real hard behind Ernie's back. I stop. And I still don't know why we're here. Ernie keeps talking about the wonders of the sea. He talks about how if the oceans die, that's the end of everything. On and on.

Ernie walks out of his office talking, with Mona at his side. I follow them for a couple of minutes through the halls of the institute. There are fish mounted in cases. Rare and beautiful. Rare and ugly. Extinct. Everything in the dark, curving halls is backlit with yellow spotlights. It's like going into the gigantic Cineplex with fifteen theaters.

I'm hypnotized and don't keep up with Mona and Ernie. I wander off into another hall and go deeper into the building—downhill—until I find myself in a long hall that's nothing but an aquarium that looks like it stretches for miles.

Even living on the water doesn't prepare me for how much I love the aquarium. I'd always managed to miss every school trip to Mystic Seaport's aquarium and every aquarium in Massachusetts.

It is magic. As magic as all the different kinds of fish and things that swim, flow, and move all over the seafloor. It takes me a few minutes to realize it isn't an aquarium, but the ocean.

The magic leaves and out of nowhere I start crying harder than I have since I threw flowers in the ocean for my brother three months ago.

When I was little, I used to throw this red-and-yellow ball out into the surf. It always came back. Mostly everything that got taken away with the waves came back. I expected it. I knew it to be true.

Red didn't come back.

He's still out there.

When Mona finds me, I am curled up on the cool stone floor, crying and hating that I ever let her bring me to this place.

"Beautiful thing?"

I don't want to talk, so I close my eyes and think of Red floating past the fish. Sailing past the seaweed and jellyfish. Drifting into the currents that took him far from here, maybe. Maybe.

Or just maybe all of a sudden right in front of me. Right here, right now. Any minute he could slowly appear in front of the smooth, cold glass. Any minute he could wave and grin at me—"It's all been one big-ass joke, Mike. I've been down here all the time, just fine. Taking a few months off from things. I was going to tell you, tell everybody, but I just got busy learning to breathe underwater."

When I look up, Mona's face is pressed against

the aquarium glass. Then her arms. Then her whole body.

I don't see Ernie around. It feels like me and Mona are the only people in the whole place.

I stand up and walk closer to Mona.

"Mona?"

Like me a few minutes ago, she doesn't want to talk. Maybe she doesn't want to hear. I understand and watch a school of fish circling some rocks, searching. . . .

I sit down right by Mona's feet and think about how much I used to feel other stuff and didn't think about aching.

21

Mona smokes and talks a mile a minute. She drives faster.

I guess we're not ready for a sea adventure. Ernie smiled real nice at us as we almost dragged each other out of the institute.

Mona throws her cigarette butt out the window and a second later slams on the brakes. Me and the car sit in the middle of the Cape road while she searches along the shoulder for her cigarette filter. She always does this. Says that those filters never break down and she must have stepped on fifty-year-old ones at the beach.

She finds it. We go.

Mona says, "I thought it was time for us to look under the water, beautiful thing."

"Yeah," I say.

"I thought if we could see . . . I thought if we could know that it wasn't so bad . . . that fish and life went on . . ."

I shake my head 'cause I don't want to hear that bull about how we all go on. The pastor said that when he held Cassie's hand, then accidentally spilled his iced tea all over the coffee table.

Frank laughed and everybody stared at him like he was insane. Then their looks changed to pity. . . .

Hell. Everybody knows that life goes on. But what kind?

22

Red,

I have always kept my promises. It's important, because what do you have if your word ain't no good? My old man says respect is the most important thing, and you get it from people if you are truthful and trustworthy. Sounds stupid to most people, I guess.

But you understand, don't you?

I miss you, man.

Your sister hurts. Mona hurts. I hurt. Can you feel our hurt?

Mona and Mike say they see you leaning against the back shed at your parents' house. They say you just stand there waiting and leaning.

Why?

What do you need from us that makes you come back? I don't want to think that you just don't know

you're not supposed to be here and are hanging around
waiting for something to happen. Are you?

I ran into your aunt Caroline the other night. She
was walking alongside the road toward me. She was
walking in the twilight with a flashlight and that long
cape she wears to freak people out. When she got about ten
feet from me, she stopped and shone the flashlight on my
shoe and said, "How long you going to walk? When are
you going to rest?"

How does she know?

Maybe she's been watching or following me through
town and along the water. I hurt, limping all over the
place.

I walked to Vedders the other day just to make sure
the car was gone, just like you wanted. Well, maybe not
just like you wanted, but it's not mine anymore.

If I could, I'd take it all back. Hand the keys over
and say, "Screw it, it's yours, man. You are my partner
and you'd love it more than me. . . ."

But I didn't.

Are you swimming now? Out in the cold, dark
water . . . Do you hear me when I scream and cry at
night? Do you know that I can't ever swim again? Not
because I'm afraid of the water, but because I'm afraid
of you.

You see, I don't know that you won't grab my legs and pull me down, down and under, forever. Would you? I wouldn't blame you if you did.

Mark

23

I've been listening again to things not spoken.

I've been quiet the last few days 'cause I'm waiting to hear.

That morning, I slept in and wrapped myself so tight in my blankets that I thought I was going to have to call for help to get me out of them. Red must have heard me twisting and grunting a minute before I rolled off the bed and banged my head on my tennis shoes.

"What's the matter with you?" he asked, laughing until he fell against my door and banged his elbow.

"What's the matter with *you* that you think me almost suffering brain damage is funny?"

"No, the rolling off the bed like some kind of

cartoon character was the funny part," he said, and ducked as I threw a pillow at him.

We didn't have many days when we got on each other's nerves, but I thought that this might be one of them. No big reason. Just a day like any other one where somebody had to get the best of somebody else.

Brothers and sisters.

24

I had spent that day swinging in a hammock but decided, after my mom looked like she was going to ask me to do some work, to hang out with Red.

He wasn't where he usually hung out (the park, Mark's, Puma's Diner). Nobody had seen him except Lyle Kramer, and who knows whether he was hallucinating or not. Lyle said he'd seen Red with Mark Hollywood, and they were hanging out at Nemo's drinking sodas and waiting for clams.

I was coming out of the toy store when Mona pulled up to the sidewalk and blew.

"Get in, beautiful thing."

I did, and we turned up the radio, singing at the top of our voices. I then drove off happy into the early summer sun, looking for Red.

We drove slowly down the Cape road until we came to the pier. Where we sat in Mona's car and watched Red and Mark leaning against Mark's sky blue '65 Mustang and remembered how all of us had stood there and watched the tall ships last summer.

Now, I can say a cool wind blew through me, but I can't say it meant anything to me then, 'cause I was standing at the edge of where I thought nothing could change.

When Red finally turned around and saw us, Mona stuck her tongue out at him. He laughed at her, then smiled at me.

moving on

25

I'm asleep and drooling on Mona's shoulder in the city jail.

I couldn't find Frank and Cassie to get Jo out, so I called Mona. We rifled through her desk (she screamed where she kept her cash as they put her in the police car) and found her bail money. Now we wait.

Malicious mischief and destruction of private property. That's what they got her for.

"Whoa!" Jo screams as we tear out of the parking lot of the Justice Center and head for Nemo's.

"Incarceration has made me hungry, girls," Jo laughs.

"How was it otherwise?" Mona asks.

"Not bad at all, not bad at all. The walls were painted peach and my cellmate had smacked a clown at some kid's party. I really liked her better than the woman who stole a bag of underwear."

"Wow," I say.

"Uh-huh," Mona sighs.

"It's not so bad going to jail. I can't believe that they caught me this time. Last time I was just a suspect," Jo says.

I lean my head out the window and take in the cool, salty breeze as we head for Nemo's. I smell fall as we pull into the parking lot and inhale fried fish. All of a sudden I'm hungry.

When I'm done with all the stuff I think I want—like traveling, finding something I can do to make some bucks, and maybe having a family—I want to be just like Jo. Her eyes sparkle and her hands move to her face and hair when she laughs. Her skin is tan and weathered from too many days on the beach. I want to swear as well as her and read poetry on my roof when I'm not planning some kind of civil disobedience (as she calls her raid on the construction site).

We sit in the booth at Nemo's with the mermaid overhead, and the lights are almost too bright as we stuff our faces with clams and lobster.

Mona and Jo laugh and eat.

I eat, watch them, and think about how easy it

is to laugh. I read somewhere that it takes less muscles to laugh than to frown. I wonder if somebody's put that on a greeting card yet.

Me and Jo sit in lawn chairs on her widow's walk.

We watch the moonlight.

The light in our living room has just come on, and I watch Cassie drop bags on the kitchen table and floor. Frank goes behind her, picking things up that have fallen out of the bag.

Cassie must be saying something funny, 'cause Frank bends over laughing, then grabs her and dances her around. A few minutes later they're kissing by the kitchen table. It makes me smile to see them kissing again. For a long time they've treated each other like brother and sister. I guess that's easier than being parents. Or at least has been for the last few months.

"I used to watch your parents dance Red around the kitchen when he was a baby. It might be three in the morning and there they'd be. Dancing. Everybody looked exhausted except him; but they danced. I don't know where they got the energy, but there they were in the middle of the night—"

"Did you ever see them dancing me?" I ask.

Jo laughs, "Honey, you were always a sleeper. It would have taken a bomb to wake you up."

"Yeah?"

"Yeah."

We listen to the ocean 'cause we can't see it anymore now that the moon has gone behind the clouds. It smells like rain, but I don't want to move off the walk. I want to hear more stories about my parents and Red. Mostly Red—but I don't know how to ask.

"He said your name first, you know. That's why you're Mike. He could never get to the other part of your name."

I smile as Jo talks through the night, telling me stories that I already know about my brother. The few I don't know make me laugh and are like secret gifts under a bed that you've been sleeping on forever and never knew anything was under.

I wake up on the lawn chaise on the widow's walk, and Jo is smoking and staring at something off in the distance. She keeps staring at whatever it is, then stops, looks at me, and nods her head.

We watch the boy by the shed dance in a pale light, and it starts to rain.

26

There was a crash thirty years ago off the bay road. A bus went right into the ocean at high tide. I often wonder how did it get all the way through the brambles and over the ditch that separates the beach from the road? I'll never know.

You can still find parts of the bus as it washes slowly, year by year, up on the beaches.

My aunt Caroline was the first person on the scene. She had watched the bus go over. She said it happened in slow motion. Like a dream.

She was seven, and she remembers it was windy the day twenty-eight people flew into beyond. And they found her standing on the edge, hair and coat blowing so wild around her that one man said she looked like some kind of witch standing there in the wind.

That's where all that witch stuff started. Caroline says that instead of fighting it, she just accepted it. It was easier, and if she imagined that there was some magic or witchcraft within her, she could control whatever she wanted. Whatever she wanted.

If I'd been a witch as I stood on that dock three months ago, I would have flown over the rocks sticking out like daggers below. I would have just skimmed the waves. I would have dived deep down past the blue gray waves and grabbed hold of my brother's hand. . . .

Now the only thing that makes me not jump in and try to grab his hand is the sure fact that— even though it would make it easier for me—I am not a witch.

I probably won't grow rosemary at my garden gate or go walking the coast road at midnight. I won't own three black cats and always know, without anybody telling me, that I'm going to have company or that somebody is sick.

I won't be able to do anything about controlling what's not in my hand.

Everybody says they saw Mark Hollywood on the Cape road hitchhiking. Strange to see him without a car. But when the school bus pulled up to give him a ride, he shook his head and wouldn't get on.

Everybody says he was walking toward the piers.

It's fall. I smelled it coming a little while ago, but it just appeared overnight in the air and trees. It's past summer blanket weather, and I've been sleeping under Red's old camp blanket, sleeping with blue beads in my hands.

And it's harder than ever now 'cause I haven't ever been without him in the fall. No season change, for that matter. Because he was here, alive, at the beginning of summer, I guess I thought if it stayed warm, I could keep him somehow.

I haven't seen Red since the night on the widow's walk. Maybe he smelled fall coming too.

Maybe it was time for him to lean and dance somewhere else.

·

27

Today I unlocked a sixth grader from a locker Pritchard Howard had put him in. It's the first time that I feel like I'm not being led by a remote control in school. It's the first day that I didn't see the whole day in front of me. I almost feel like something could happen that I haven't already been through.

I almost feel like I'm pulling myself out of a too-hot bath that makes you tired and sleepy, and almost pass out before you can get to a chair.

The kid is pretty shaky. Gia comes up to us and offers to walk the kid back to where he belongs. She smiles at me like an old friend. Then I remember, she was and probably still is.

Mona is standing in the door of the gym, looking. She holds a pack of cigarettes in her hand. I can't tell if she wants to smoke them or throw them away. Finally, though, she puts them in her sweatshirt pocket, turns around, sees me, and shrugs.

"Hey, beautiful thing."

"Hey."

"Where you going? Not to class, I hope?" she smiles.

I say, "Since I'm here . . ."

"Hell, beautiful thing, we can't go by that. We can always change our minds and not be here. We could be anywhere else but here."

"I guess so," I say.

"I know so."

I lean against a poster the cheerleaders have put up announcing a bake sale.

"I can stand it here. It's not so bad, I guess."

Mona smiles, looks around, and takes out a cigarette. She doesn't light it, but her shoulders go down when it's between her lips.

"I can't stand it. I can't stand expecting him to walk around a corner laughing. I can't stand sitting in the lunchroom expecting him to walk up behind me and take some of my food. And I sure as hell can't take the way everybody stops talking about whatever they're talking about when I come around."

Mona sits down in front of the gym and lights up, smiling at me. She's still sitting there when I walk away and a teacher comes up and tells her to put it out, which of course, she doesn't.

The pots on Mark's front porch are all gone. He hates mums, so the porch is just lonely and colorless.

He sits on the steps, scratching underneath his cast with a long piece of bamboo.

It's funny the happy look he gets on his face when he hits the itch. I sit down beside him, letting my book bag tumble down the stairs.

Mark looks surprised. "Books?"

"Yeah, books."

"Damn. That's a good thing, huh?"

"I guess," I say.

Then I lean against Mark and he leans against me.

28

Mona's gone.

Before she took off, she stopped by Caroline's house. They hardly knew each other, but Caroline says she just opened the door and came right in.

They didn't say anything to each other, then Caroline got up from the kitchen table and made some tea.

They still didn't talk, just sipped tea and looked out the window, Caroline says.

Then Mona hugged her and left.

Now I'm here at Caroline's, sitting where Mona sat. But I won't be silent. It's time for me to tell it.

All of it.

Red holds Mona in his arms but keeps on smiling at me.

Mark stands up on the hood of his car.

Red says, "Hey, man, that's my car. You gonna dent it or what?"

"It's yours when you do the deed, dude."

"Are you gonna do it this time?" Mona says, then kisses Red until he laughs.

"Oh, yeah, the tide's just right."

I sit down on the edge of the pier and dangle my feet. I dream of jumping into the foamy white water and missing the rocks.

It can be done. People do it all the time, and Red and Mark made the deal a long time ago. Red would get the car if he jumped and swam out to the buoy.

No problem when the tide is right. No problem.

Mona holds Red's boots and blue bead necklace.

It's quiet on the pier when he dives off, and we all scream and laugh (even Mark) when he misses the rocks and starts swimming out to the buoy. When he makes it, Mona grabs me and I get excited about having the car. Mark shakes his head and rubs the hood of his car with his T-shirt.

He says, "Bye, baby," to his car as we wait for Red to swim back and make the slow climb up the pier.

Halfway back to us, though, he disappears.

We never see him again. That easy. That fast. That gone.

I don't tell Caroline how we had to hold Mark back from jumping into the rocks, or how I couldn't move and thought I'd never stop screaming. I don't tell her how Mona climbed down the pier and almost drowned herself. Looking for Red.

Caroline says, "Mona couldn't cry on the boat. I remember. She held herself real close and tight, and the only people she'd even let get close to her were you and Mark."

I say, "Uh-huh."

Caroline pulls me close and says, "How long were you all going to suffer with this?"

I look over her shoulder through the big picture window out to the ocean.

"Forever," I say. "Always and forever."

After the all of it I leave Caroline, and I walk slowly down the drive and listen to the ocean pound against the shore. As always.

29

I had a dream last night that the old fisherman Red was standing underneath my window. He just stood and stared up at the house like he was waiting for somebody to come out.

A few minutes later Red was standing beside him, but they were both in the dark. There was no soft light cradling them and making me feel better.

There was no dancing or leaning against anything to make you think they were waiting. They just watched. Then after a while they walked away.

I can't remember a time when I didn't think it would always be me on the back of my brother's bike. I can't remember a time when I said, "Take me," and he didn't.

When I walk on the beach now, it's bitter cold

and I wear Red's ski cap and his sunglasses. The gulls sweep down and call to one another. It can't ever be that way for Red and me, but I'm going to stay here. I want to be here.

Not just because I can't leave Red, but because I feel him here. I'm not saying I won't leave the Cape; but I know I will always come back.

Always.

And then the light starts changing in the sky, and I see Cassie and Frank watching out the window for me. I wonder if they see me the way I see myself now.

Not the same. Never the same; but another way altogether.

Read Cynthia Voigt's acclaimed Tillerman cycle
from beginning to end:

HOMECOMING
"An enthralling journey to a gratifying end."
—*New York Times Book Review*

DICEY'S SONG
Winner of the Newbery Medal

A SOLITARY BLUE
A Newbery Honor Book

THE RUNNER

COME A STRANGER

SONS FROM AFAR

SEVENTEEN AGAINST THE DEALER

POWERFUL FICTION FROM
AWARD-WINNING AUTHOR
JAMES HOWE

THE WATCHER
0-689-80186-6 (hardcover)
0-689-82662-1 (trade paperback)
0-689-83533-7 (rack)
An ALA Quick Pick for Young Adults
An ALA Best Book for Young Adults

THE MISFITS
0-689-83955-3 (hardcover)
0-689-83956-1 (paperback)

Edited by James Howe
THE COLOR OF ABSENCE
0-689-82862-4 (hardcover)
0-689-85667-9 (paperback)

Aladdin Paperbacks/Simon Pulse
Simon & Schuster Children's Publishing
www.SimonSays.com

Award-winning fiction by
Virginia Hamilton.

The House of Dies Drear
**Mystery Writers of America's
Edgar Award**
0-02-043520-7

The Planet of Junior Brown
A Newbery Honor book
0-02-043540-1 (Rack)
0-689-71721-0 (Digest)

Zeely
ALA Notable Book of the Year
0-689-71695-8

MC Higgins, the Great
**Winner of the Newbery Medal
Winner of the National Book Award**
0-02-043490-1 (Rack)
0-689-71694-X (Digest)